The Adventures of

Lifeboat LUKE

Rubberduckadoo

Straandlooper
ANIMATION

Appletree Press

Snoring and snoozing and Donaghadoo's in
the deep of the night and the moon's silver light.

Sssssssshh! What's that?

Gannet's awakened and Mona looks shaken,
by spooky-most screakling!

I hope I'm mistaken!
Screeaaakkkk!!

Eyes! Huge and unblinking, not merry and twinkling...

but starey and scary – oh Mona be wary – Get Help!

They're off towards D'oo
with a squawk and a poo!

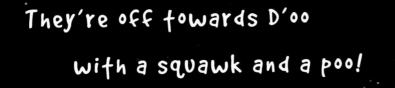

Well they're frightened –
what else did you think they would do?

Oh dear!!

What's that?

All black and bobbly - poor Brendan looks wobbly.

I'm scared – it's all glisteny–
don't hang around listening.

Find Luke!!

There he is napping happily
waves gently lappily -

friends in a panic – Honk! Whistle! and Flappily –

Pleeeeaaaase! WAKE UP!

A ship on the rocks? A man in wet socks?
I don't think my nerves can take any more shocks!

Mummmmyyyy!!!

Hooray! Luke's away
in the dark of the day
– I mean night.

It won't take him long before everything wrong is put right.

Go Lukey!!

That ship's on the rocks
and it's sinking I think...

...and the deck of the wreck
will be dunked in the drink.

Come on Luke!!

BANG!
Going down like a brick...
Hokey Fyfe!!
I feel sick, I can't look!

Note: Breeches Buoy is a cable linking the ship to the lifeboat that carries a person in a big pair of safety knickers, and if you knew that I'll eat mine! – joke

Eyes Again!

Cold and staring – with hard white light flaring,
and the screakling and squeaking it's horribly scaring.

WHAT ARE THEY?!!

What? Ha! Me - scared of those?

Well well well - bless my nose!

I could laugh from my head to the tips of my toes -

RUBBER DUCKS!

To think you were frightened!
Well now you're enlightened!

You'll see they are ducks

now the dawn sky has brightened.

Jefferson Airplane!

Ducks jiggling jogglingly!

Luke has one - Mona and
Brendan and YOU have one,

Gannet and Ardal and –

I WANT ONE TOO!

Will you lend me yours please if I beg on my knees,
the next time you're passing through Donaghadoo?

Toodle-oo!

First published in 2009 by
Appletree Press Ltd.,
The Old Potato Station, 14 Howard Street South,
Belfast. BT7 1AP

Published in association with
Straandlooper Limited,
128a High Street, Holywood, County Down, BT18 9HW
Northern Ireland.

Text and images © 2008 Luke the Lifeboat Ltd.
Based on original designs by Alastair McIlwain.
Illustrations compiled by Stuart Wilkinson and Dean Burke from the television series.
Text by Richard Morss.

A catalogue record for this book is available from the British Library.

The Adventures of Lifeboat Luke: Rubberduckadoo
www.lifeboatluke.tv

ISBN: 978 1 84758 142 6

9 8 7 6 5 4 3 2 1